This book is dedicated to
Beth and Shaun
(down under!)

Text and illustrations copyright © Keith Brumpton 2001
Book copyright © Hodder Wayland 2001

Published in Great Britain in 2001
by Hodder Wayland, an imprint of
Hodder Children's Books

British Library Cataloguing in Publication Data
Brumpton, Keith
 The Sword in the Scone. – (Super Stars)
 1. Children's Stories
 I. Title
 823.9'14 [J]

ISBN: 0 7502 3213 7 HB
ISBN: 0 7502 3214 5 PB

Printed in Hong Kong by Wing King Tong

Hodder Children's Books
A division of Hodder Headline Limited
338 Euston Road, London NW1 3BH

keith brumpton

The Sword in the Scone

YE TITLE PAGE

HODDER
Wayland

an imprint of Hodder Children's Books

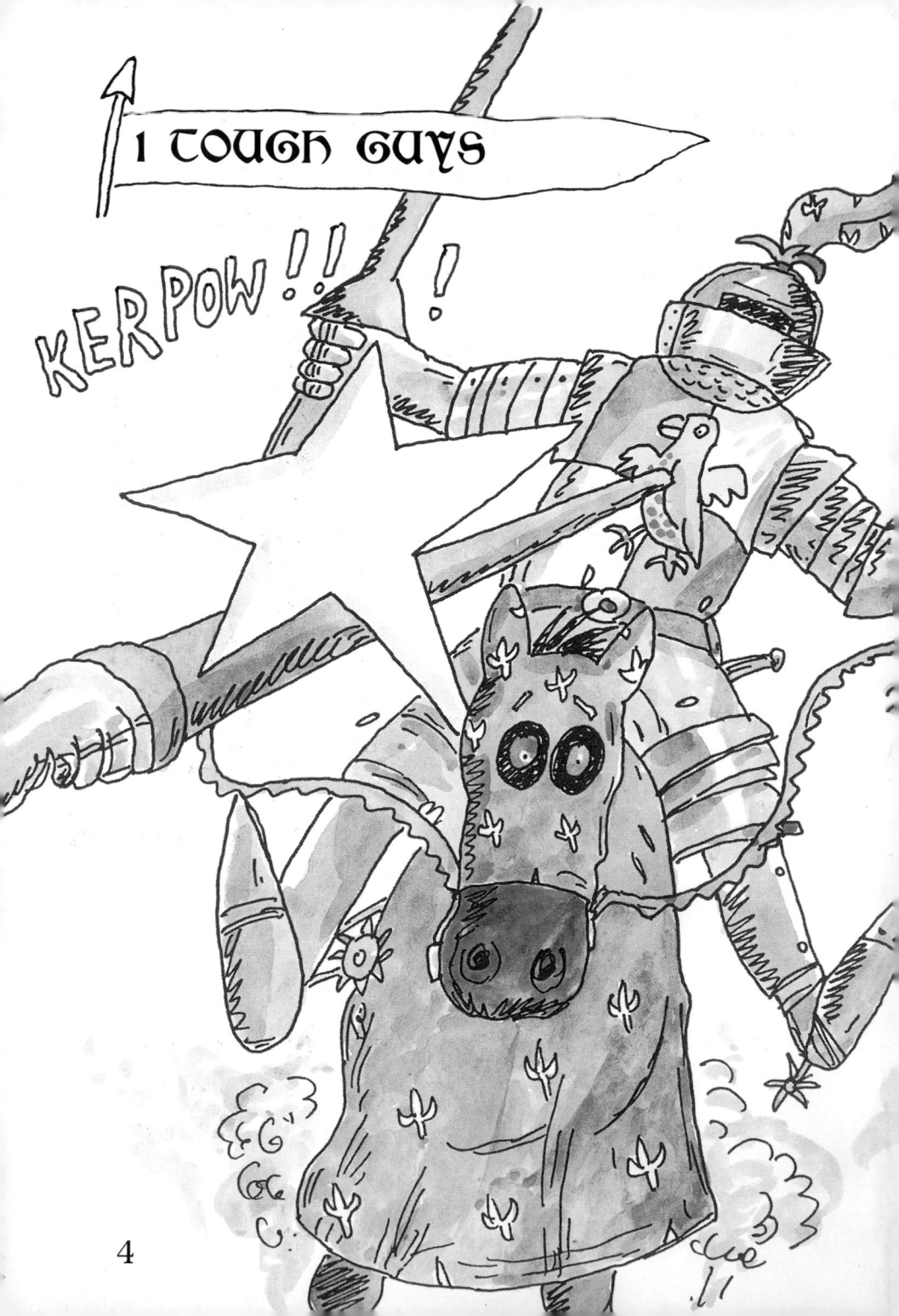

"Well, it's all beyond me," grumbled Beowulf, the enchanted dog. "Why would anyone find it interesting to watch two grown men charging into each other whilst carrying bits of wood?"

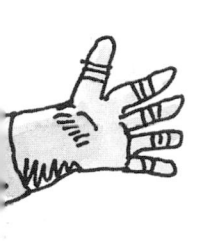

He and Owen were watching the big jousting tournament, held each year in the castle grounds.

Owen was only a humble serf, so he wasn't allowed to take part in the games. Jousting was only for the rich and powerful knights such as Sir Lance Allott, Sir Nobrayne, and the crowd's favourite, Saracen Ford.

5

"I just don't get the point," said Beowulf.

Owen wished that one day *he* could take part in the big tournament. He imagined himself galloping into the arena (on a horse, preferably), to be greeted by the roar of the crowd. Perhaps the ladies of the court would be wearing his colours, instead of Sir Lance Allott's? Owen sighed loudly.

Beowulf looked up and gave a growl. "You're well out of it. Horses aren't to be trusted, you know... Bad breath, bad temper, and nothing up top."

Sir Lance Allott had just unseated his opponent, Sir Giles Twitzgibbon. It seemed to Owen that Sir Lance's lance was longer than anyone else's. But that would be cheating and surely a Knight of the Round Table and Matching Chairs would never do that?

After the tournament, Owen and Beowulf walked back across the muddy fields to the hovel where Owen lived. A raven flew overhead. Then it turned back and landed on a branch beside them.

What does _he_ want?

Owen had a feeling that the bird was going to speak. Since Merlin had become court magician there were a lot of strange spells about:

"I've got a message from Merlin," began the raven. "Though why he didn't send a pigeon is beyond me. It's not like I haven't got better things to do."

"The message?" asked Owen.

"Oh, yes, sorry. He wants to meet you later."

"What time?"

Midday outside the swordsmiths.

Malcolm the raven gave a croak and took off. In no time at all he'd left Owen and Beowulf far behind and was within sight of the tall, turreted tower where Merlin lived. He slipped in through a tiny slit window and hopped on to the arm of the chair in which his master lay dozing.

"Well then, is the deed done?" Merlin asked, opening one eye in Malcolm's direction.

"Sure is, pointy-hat. We're meeting Owen at the swordsmiths' at midday."

Merlin rose unsteadily to his feet and went over to his crystal ball.

Merlin peered into the ball. It was as cloudy as a bank holiday weekend, but gradually the mists began to clear. He could see Owen.

"One day that boy will be king," said Merlin. "But only if we can keep him safe. The first thing we need to do is to find him a weapon with which to fight."

"Good weapons cost money and he earns even less than we do," croaked Malcolm.

"So we'll have to help him out," mumbled Merlin, determinedly. "Now, let's get ready for our meeting…"

2 Masters Sharp and Blunt

Owen was waiting outside the entrance to
the swordsmiths'. It was a cold November day,
so he was glad of the warmth from the anvil,
glowing within.

Sharp and Blunt was the best swordsmiths' in all of Camelot. All the top knights used to shop there, from Sir Ivan Ho-Ho to Saracen Ford. Owen, being a lowly peasant boy, had never been able to afford one of their swords. And without a sword, he could never become a knight.

Master Sharp saw Owen loitering outside and came out for a friendly word.

Push off, peasant boy!

"I'm waiting for Merlin," muttered Owen, not wanting to pick a fight with this man mountain.

Beowulf bared his teeth, ready for action.

Just in time, Merlin arrived.

Master Sharp gave the wizard an evil stare. "You mean to buy this urchin a sword?"

Merlin was looking in his silk purse. There didn't seem to be many coins in there. "How much would a sword cost, exactly?"

Master Sharp waved them into his workshop.
A number of swords were hanging on the wall.
"It depends what you want of course… you've
got your top of the range models like your
'Kingslayer' and your 'Visorsplicer'."

Master Sharp pointed to another set of
swords, lower down the wall. "Well, in the
mid-range there's the 'Slashman 500'. That
comes in at about eight gold crowns."

Merlin looked a little pale. "*Eight* gold
crowns?" he squeaked. "Er, what's the
cheapest sword you do?"

The burly swordsmith spat out of the side of his mouth and looked down at Owen...

Mmm... Not bad!

"For a little shrimp like this you could try the 'Squire'. That's three gold crowns. Good for a beginner, comes with its own scabbard and a five-battle guarantee."

Merlin felt in his purse again. He had only two
gold coins.

"Timewasters!" muttered Master Sharp,
wandering off to bash some more metal.

Merlin laid a hand on Owen's shoulder. "I'm sorry, lad, I had no idea a good sword was so expensive these days."

"That's OK, Merlin. I'll start saving."

A thoughtful look suddenly crossed the old magician's face. "There *is* one other way we might get you a sword…" He reached into his robes and pulled out a crumpled sheet of parchment. Owen's eyes lit up.

The poster showed the most famous sword in Camelot, the legendary Excalibur.

You'd like to know more about the legend? OK. Read on…

3 The Excalibur Files

Excalibur was a magic sword, given to King Arthur by the Lady of the Lake. (She also gave him a book token and a set of stick-on shield transfers, but no one talks about that.)

Arthur had many years of happy use out of Excalibur. He used it to slay dragons, to behead his enemies, and to chop pastry into pretty shapes.

But then, one fateful day, he flung Excalibur away whilst in a fit of rage, and it landed in an enchanted scone. Now no one, not even the king himself, could draw Excalibur from this scone.

The legend grew and grew, like a giant's toenail. It was said that whosoever could draw the sword from the giant scone would get to keep the sword and would one day succeed Arthur as king...

Merlin was still looking at the piece of
parchment. "You know that each year there's
a contest to try and pull the sword from the
scone? Imagine if you were to win Excalibur?
That would be the perfect sword for a
young squire!"

Malcolm the raven gave a croak. "And imagine if pigs could fly and Queen Guinevere grew a beard…"

Owen scratched his head. "It's quite a prize. I don't ever want to be king, but I'd love to own a real sword."

Beowulf wagged his tail. "No harm in giving it a go."

Merlin continued reading and learned that the Sword-pulling Challenge was to take place later that same week, and that entries had to be in by noon the next day. He made a note in his diary and wondered if the youngster was ready for such a challenge.

4 Sir Lance Works Out

Sir Lance Allott was running round the courtyard of the castle. It was his third lap and beneath his helmet things were getting very hot and sweaty.

Sir Nobrayne looked at the hourglass on his wrist and shouted to his friend. "Eight minutes, thirty-three seconds. You're slowing down!"

"I'll slow *you* down," growled Sir Lance Allott. "It isn't easy running in full armour, you know."

"Why are we doing this again?" asked Sir Nobrayne, who oddly enough had almost no brain at all.

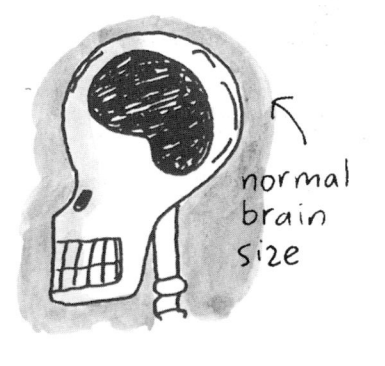

normal brain size

Sir Nobrayne's brain size

Sir Lance Allott gave an exasperated sigh. "Because it's the Sword-pulling Challenge in three days' time and I, I mean we, want to win Excalibur, become king, and kill everyone except Queen Guinevere and all the girls."

"And ourselves. We wouldn't want to kill ourselves, would we?" asked Sir Nobrayne.

Give me strength!

At the end of his fifth lap, Sir Lance Allott collapsed in a heap of steaming metal. It was his bad luck that the queen and Princess Katherine chose that same moment to walk past, exercising their pet dragon, Damien.

"Sir Lance Allott looks a little out of shape these days," laughed the queen.

"Yes, not like that Saracen Ford," added Princess Katherine.

"You should try doing some exercises, Lance," suggested the queen, helpfully.

The two ladies walked on, giggling, leaving Sir Nobrayne to help his friend to his feet again. It wasn't easy in all that heavy armour.

"Is Saracen Ford *really* that fit?" asked Sir Nobryane.

No match for us! He's all mouth and no leg armour.

Meanwhile, in the Castle gym...

More weights, serf!

Saracen Ford

Saracen Ford was most people's favourite to win the contest.

Surely if anyone was strong enough to wrench Excalibur from the stale pastry, it would be him?

Saracen had no need of the sword. He already had a nice little scimitar.

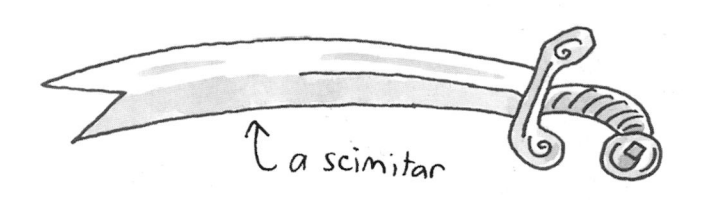

↳ a scimitar

What he really wanted to do was to succeed Arthur as king. Saracen was an ambitious man with all sorts of evil plans for boiling people in oil, and fighting lots of wars in lots of different places and filling his pockets.

If *he* won the contest, it would be a disaster for Camelot. Little wonder that King Arthur's face wore a worried frown…

The storm clouds are gathering over our little Kingdom!

It's sure wet out there!

5 Gathering Clouds

Inside Merlin's castle, Malcolm was spluttering, "Er, the magic phoenix is on fire again."

Merlin doused the troublesome bird and returned to his crystal ball...

The crystal ball seemed to grow larger, the glass acting like a magnifying glass until Merlin could see everything as clear as daylight...

Owen, meanwhile, was in a field, watching over a flock of sheep, which was one of his many duties. He also had with him a toy sword made from wood, which from time to time he practised pulling out of a muddy bank.

34

Hidden from view, sheltered behind a large and twisted chestnut tree, stood Sir Lance Allott and Sir Nobrayne. They were watching Owen and planning dark deeds.

"He might enter the competition. He is young and strong," muttered Sir Lance Allott to Sir Nobrayne.

Sir Lance Allott was always one for a cunning plan and today was no exception. "How long would it take a boy and a dog to round up all those sheep?" he asked.

A very long time?

Exactly!

Sir Lance Allott sliced through the timber fence with his sword (a Kingslayer 5000), then watched with glee as Sir Nobrayne drove the sheep out of the field and into the surrounding woods.

By the time Owen noticed anything it was too
late. One-hundred-and-twenty-eight sheep had
scattered to the hills. Beowulf raced after them
but there wasn't much he could do except bark.

Beowulf wasn't as trusting as Owen, and he had a better sense of smell, too. He recognized Sir Lance Allott's aftershave and Sir Nobrayne's lack-of-shave...

But he knew there was no point in worrying about it for now. Their first priority was to catch those sheep before dark.

Owen didn't get much sleep that night. It wasn't exactly ideal preparation for the Sword-pulling Challenge.

By dawn the next day, Owen was still two sheep short of a flock. There was now no chance he could get to the castle in time to deliver his entry form for the Sword-pulling Challenge.

Beowulf offered to run on ahead with the form between his teeth, but Owen was worried about what Sir Lance Allott and some of the knights might do to his beloved wolfhound.

So they spent a sad morning rounding up the last of the woollybacks and dreaming of what might have been...

It was five to noon and two yellow pages were
collecting entry forms from Camelot's top
knights.

Sir Nobrayne rode under the portcullis, forgot to duck his head, and was knocked into the moat. High up in her royal bedroom, Princess Katherine burst into laughter. She thought Sir Nobrayne was the silliest of her knights and wouldn't have much chance of winning the contest.

43

She watched him drying off his entry form and then handing it over. Alongside stood Sir Lance Allott and Sir Gallopahead. Saracen Ford was striding up and down, accompanied by a couple of his squires. He pushed Sir Lance Allott and Sir Lance Allott pushed back.

The knights were getting very excited down there. So excited that no one noticed a tall figure in black scurry through the castle gates...

7 Countdown

Entries to the contest had closed. Arthur and Guinevere were in the castle dungeon. The queen was doing some decorating.

"Yes. Why do you ask?"

"Oh, no reason. Just he looks the sort of muscly, powerful chap who'd do very well."

Arthur arranged the entries in the order they'd been received. There was only one name he didn't recognize. "Terrible handwriting. Should be disqualified really. Don't know what they teach them in school these days."

"We don't have any schools, dear."

8 Knights Pullover

Saracen Ford was wearing his finest helmet.
"How do I look?" he asked his squire. "Do
I look like a king?"

His squire nodded. (So would you if you were
asked that sort of question by a heavily armed
Saracen psychopath.)

"You look the business, Master."

Saracen twirled his moustache with pride.

And remember...

"...the moment I pull the sword from the scone I want you to grab hold of the king and queen. With them as my hostages, no one will dare resist."

I'll be the King of Camelot, and all England will fall at my feet...

You don't think the other helmet looks better?

Lots of the local peasantry had gathered outside the castle to watch the contest. It was always a big event. To entertain the crowd there were jugglers, minstrels, dancing bears and a storytelling monk.

Why did the peasant cross the drawbridge? *

That really is another story.

Owen made himself comfortable on a grassy bank, next to Beowulf. It was a fine, sunny day. Owen was just about to close his eyes, exhausted by the labours of the past few days, when a familiar figure in black strode into view, accompanied by Malcolm the raven.

No time to sleep, lad... You have to get ready.

Owen tried to explain about the lost sheep and not having had time to submit his entry form.

"Oh, don't worry about that. I put in an entry on your behalf."

Yes, dear reader. I was the mystery figure at the bottom of page 44!

"Look, here come the other contestants!" said Malcolm.

Four strong serfs had lowered the sword and scone into position, in front of the gaily decorated pavilion where the king and queen and ladies of the court were already seated. The pavilion was covered with the banners of each of the Knights of the Round Table and Matching Chairs: Sir Lance Allott's lion, the crossed scimitars of Saracen Ford, and the two rampant budgies of Sir Nobrayne. Every knight was taking part, apart from two: Sir Burnham (off fighting dragons) and Sir Percival (hamstring injury).

"Let the joust begin!" announced the king.

Everyone looked puzzled.

"Er, sorry… let the Sword-pulling begin," he continued.

The queen dropped her silk handkerchief.

"You've dropped your hankie, dear," said the king.

"I know. That's the signal to start the contest."

Is it really? No one tells me anything!

9 Tug! Tug Hard, Sire

Sir Twitzherbert was the first to try pulling the sword from the scone. He managed to move it about 1.2 millimetres, then gave up, exhausted. One by one, each of the knights took their turn. Sir Nobrayne collapsed with a bad back. Sir Ivan Ho-Ho sprained his ankle.

And then came the big guns... Saracen Ford was confident. Very confident. He battled to draw Excalibur until the veins on his head stood out and the sweat dribbled down his chain mail.

For eighteen long minutes he fought the
sword, before retiring with an angry scowl.

Next up was Sir Lance Allott. He, too, was
confident, but he didn't last long. An old
shoulder injury seemed to trouble him right
from the start.
Even a quick
massage from the
queen couldn't
help. He, too, was
forced to give up.

The serfs were just about to carry Excalibur away for another year when Merlin gave a little cough. "There is, I believe, one more contestant?"

The king consulted his notes. "Ah, yes, the name I didn't recognize. The badly written one. *Irwin?*"

"Owen, Your Highness. Owen Duckworth. One of your servant lads," said Merlin.

Sir Lance Allott went red in the face.

"Impossible, Your Highness!" spluttered Sir Lance Allott. "This contest is only for Knights of the Round Table and Matching Chairs."

Princess Katherine looked at the rules.

"That's where you're wrong, Sir Lance... Listen... 'This challenge will be open to anyone in ye kingdom, be they lord or lady, serf or slave...' "

"Don't worry," whispered Sir Nobrayne to his no-good friend. "The lad has no chance. I've seen more muscles on a... on a..." He couldn't think of anything that didn't have muscles. "Well he doesn't have a chance, anyway!"

Most people in the crowd seemed to share his opinion. There was a lot of laughter and sniggering as Owen nervously strode forward. He felt like turning back but Merlin gave him a little wink of encouragement and Beowulf was there, too, wagging his tail.

57

Owen stood in front of the great sword, which was almost as tall as him. The faint rays of the morning sun gleamed off its silvery handle and dazzled his eyes. He took a deep breath. His mouth felt dry. The crowd were silent now. In the distance a bird sang. Owen felt the icy-cold sword handle in the palm of his hands and pulled, slowly.

He expected nothing to happen, waited for the sound of the crowd's laughter, but it never came.

Instead he found the sword moving smoothly, like a dragon through water, until the whole blade, the great Excalibur, lay exposed, reflecting in the rays of the sun. Dazzle-bright! Owen had drawn the sword from the scone!

10 Arise, Owen Gets a Rise

As well as winning Excalibur, Owen was now the proud owner of fifty crowns' worth of tokens for *Sharp and Blunt*. Fifty crowns would buy him some accessories for his sword – a decent shield and maybe a helmet, too. Owen's next big task was to design a coat of arms to put on his shield...

Princess Katherine suggested a portrait of herself and some checked colours in her favourite shade of red. Queen Guinevere thought her favourite flower, a rose, would be nice.

Owen was tempted to please the ladies but in the end he knew what he wanted on his shield. It featured neither princesses nor dragons, nor any of the usual things. Owen's coat of arms included a magician's hat and wand, and the head of a dog... A wolfhound, to be precise!

Owen was sitting on the hillside beneath a shower of shooting stars. Excalibur lay on the ground beside him. Beowulf lay his head in Owen's lap and together they dreamed of new adventures... of dungeons and dragons and faraway places, of jousting, tasty boncs... (actually that was just Beowulf).

"Baaa!"

There was still a flock of sheep to look after, though!

Ye ende

Look out for these other titles in the Super Stars range:

The Green Knight by Keith Brumpton
Princess Katherine has run away (again) and she has strayed into
the realm of the evil Green Knight. King Arthur has put up a
reward (an attractive luggage set) for the princess's safe return.
Who will save her – Sir Lance Allott or Owen Duckworth and his
trusty hound, Beowulf? Or will the Green Knight get there first?

Superheroes Down the Plughole by Keith Brumpton
Elasticman, Mothgirl and the others have lost their powers...
When they learn that the Superhero Inspectorate is coming to
check them out, the pressure is on. Can our clapped-out crew of
caped crusaders prove once and for all that they really are still
superheroes?

You can buy all these books from your local bookseller,
or order them direct from the publisher. For more information
about Super Stars, write to: *The Sales Department, Hodder
Children's Books, a division of Hodder Headline Limited,
338 Euston Road, London NW1 3BH.*